First published in Great Britain in 2020 by Andersen Press Ltd.,
20 Vauxhall Bridge Road, London SW1V 2SA.
Copyright © Fred Blunt 2020. The right of Fred Blunt to be identified
as the author and illustrator of this work has been asserted by him
in accordance with the Copyright, Designs and Patents Act, 1988.
All rights reserved. Printed and bound in China.
10 9 8 7 6 5 4 3 2 1
British Library Cataloguing in Publication Data available.
ISBN 978 1 78344 868 5

Fred BLunT

Gnome

Ⓐ

Andersen Press

This little fellow is a gnome.

Say hello to the readers, Mr Gnome.

Ah - fishing! Gnomes like fishing.
Can we join in?

You're not very friendly.

We'd better not disturb Mr Gnome while he's fishing.

Oh look, here comes a hedgehog.

He's got an apple stuck on his spines.
Poor Mr Hedgehog.

Isn't Mr Hedgehog polite?

You're not polite, Mr Gnome.

Oh, that wasn't very nice, Mr Gnome.
Didn't you want to help that kind, polite hedgehog?

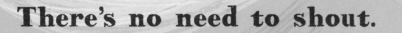

There's no need to shout.

Who's this coming along,
eating Hedgehog's juicy red apple?
Is it a witch?

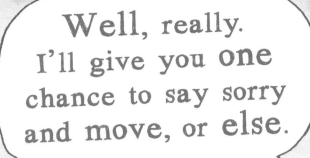

Mr. Gnome might be making a big mistake...

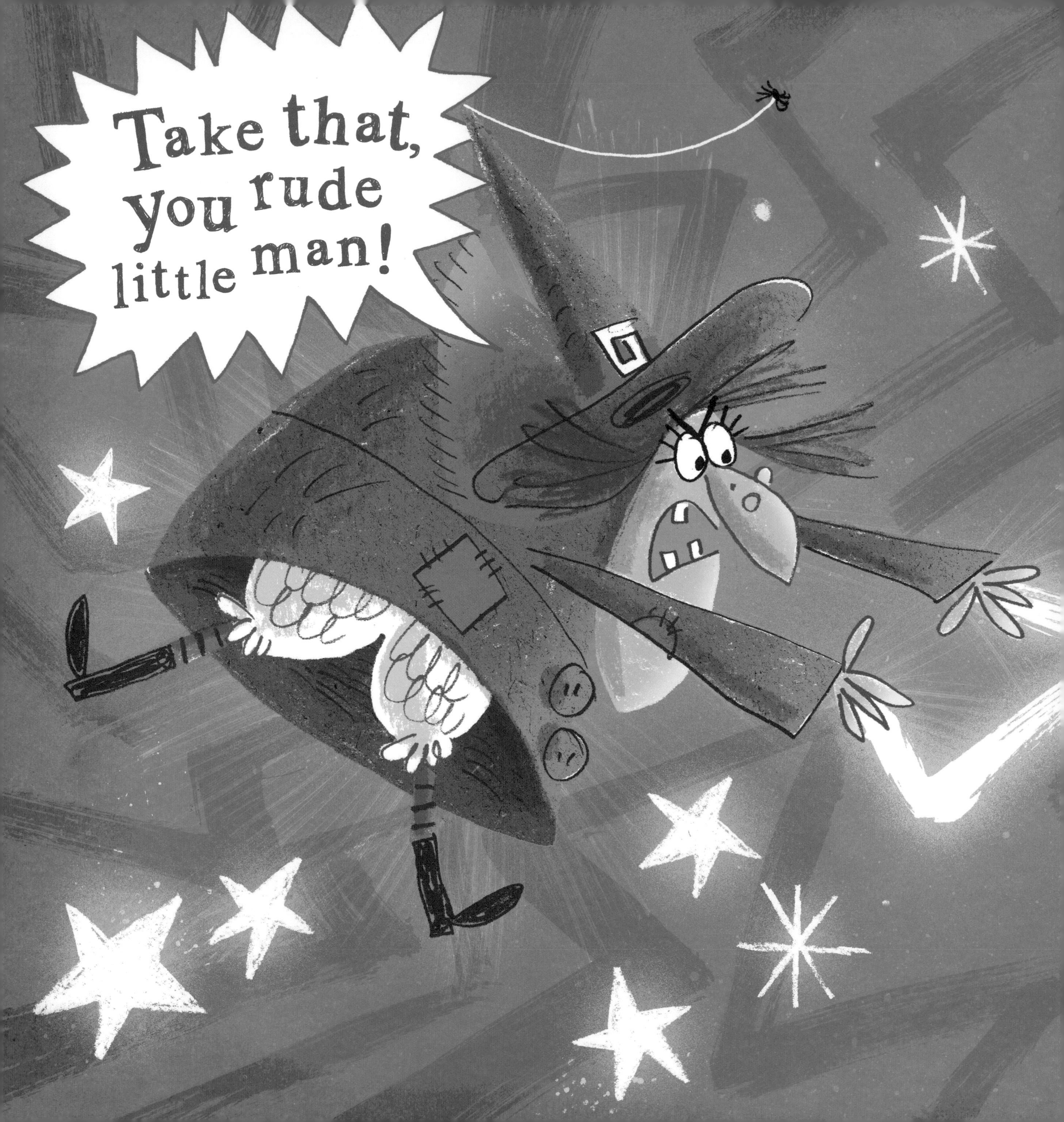
Take that, you rude little man!

Oh dear, Mr Gnome
has been turned to stone.

Oops, bet he's sorry now.

Whatever does she mean?

Wow!
That's a fine collection
of gnomes you have,
Miss Witch!

Maybe Mr Gnome has learnt his lesson now?

Could you change him back, please?

Please, please, please?

Well, well, well. So now we know...

where the garden
gnome comes from!

The End